SHERMAN'S ANGELS

A CHRISTMAS STORY

To Avriel,

Merry Christmas!

Gary T Green

SHERMAN'S ANGELS

A CHRISTMAS STORY

GARY J GRIECO

TATE PUBLISHING
AND **ENTERPRISES**, LLC

Published by Tate Publishing & Enterprises, LLC
127 E. Trade Center Terrace | Mustang, Oklahoma 73064 USA
1.888.361.9473 | www.tatepublishing.com

Tate Publishing is committed to excellence in the publishing industry. The company reflects the philosophy established by the founders, based on Psalm 68:11,
"The Lord gave the word and great was the company of those who published it."

Book design copyright © 2014 by Tate Publishing, LLC. All rights reserved.
Cover design by Rtor Maghuyop
Interior design by Joana Quilantang
Artwork provided by John Grabar, an accomplished cartoonist residing in Cheshire, Connecticut.

Published in the United States of America

ISBN: 978-1-63185-741-6
1. Fiction / Biographical
2. Fiction / War & Military
14.08.12

Acknowledgments

I am grateful to all those who have offered
encouragement and advice, including especially:
My loving wife, Sarah;
My first editor, Caroline Danielson;
My friend and fellow survivor of Brother Edmund's
sophomore English class, Joseph Appierto.

Foreword

This coming Christmas season marks the 150th anniversary of General Sherman's Savannah Campaign, popularly known as Sherman's March to the Sea. It is a controversial and disturbing chapter in American history. The Federal army's lack of respect for life and property while slashing a mortal wound across our Southern states has been painstakingly documented in Civil War history books. But acts of great compassion can also be found, buried deep within these military narratives, if one searches diligently enough.

This story is about good people, people of faith who fought to maintain their moral values during one of our country's darkest hours. They then fought to soothe their souls after the battles were done.

May we all celebrate the Christmas season with joy, good fellowship, and spiritual renewal. And may we also take time to reflect upon and honor those brave soldiers of a bygone era who fought and died for the abolishment of slavery and the reunification of our nation.

—Gary J. Grieco

Chapter 1

Central Indiana, Christmas Eve, 1888

No one should have to bury a loved one on Christmas Eve. "In the sweat of thy face shalt thou eat bread, till thou return unto the ground; for out of it was thou taken: for dust thou art, and unto dust shalt thou return."

Mary and Becky, huddled together in a softly falling snowfall, looked on quietly as their adoption mother's mortal remains were lowered into the cold ground of Sycamore Hill Cemetery. Beatrice Hamilton was laid to rest alongside her husband, Isaac, who had passed away a quarter of a century earlier. Having lived a full life, she embraced eternity in her final hours with the strength only faith can provide.

Graveside prayers were short and standard, owing to a frigid breeze and Parson Fletcher's lack of imagination. They were fortunate, the cemetery worker had told them, as it had been a mild start to winter, and so frozen earth hadn't prevented a grave from being dug. This was a strange blessing, but a comfort to all, nonetheless.

After the service concluded, Mary, her twin sister Becky, and Robert, Becky's husband of less than a year, stood quietly together to the sheltered side of the cemetery's hill, pondering what they were to do next. Plans for the evening had not been made and darkness was fast approaching. All this changed when Aunt Gertrude and Uncle Zeke approached them.

"Girls, you must come to my house and we'll have a quiet Christmas Eve dinner. Your mother would have wanted it this way. You mustn't spend the evening by yourselves. Agreed? We are all in agreement, then!"

Not pausing for a response, which was Aunt Gertrude's style, she continued on, having barely taken a breath.

"The graveside service was just awful, wasn't it? Parson Fletcher knew your mother all these many years and she attended his service every Sunday, and yet he couldn't find it in him to say just one nice word about her? All he did was read from a prayer book. Well I'll have a thing or two to say to him tomorrow after Christmas service!"

Pity the parson. The wrath of Aunt Gertrude, delivered by her sharp tongue and shrill voice, has been likened to a hailstorm in a hurricane, if such a meteorological event is at all possible. The most frequent target of Aunt Gertrude's sharp tongue was her husband, Ezekiel. Uncle Zeke, a sad looking gentleman, short in stature with a nearly bald head compensated for by a droopy white mustache, had been rendered nearly speechless by her onslaught. Rumor had it that Uncle Zeke hadn't strung together two consecutive sentences since he returned home from the Great Civil War.

"We'll be pleased to join you for dinner, Aunt Gertrude," responded Becky, much to her sister Mary's surprise.

"Good, then you girls should just ride right over to the house. If you arrive before we do, stoke the fire and make yourselves comfortable."

Aunt Gertrude hadn't accepted Robert into the family yet, and she always made it a point to ignore him in social situations, other than the occasional hello or good-bye. To Robert's credit, he embraced his lowly status in Aunt Gertrude's pecking order. Most folks considered him quite the fortunate one.

"And don't worry about your not bringing anything—I have enough food for everyone. I just haven't been able to get in there and start cooking yet. Zeke! Are you ready to take me home? It's as cold as cold can be out here! This old thin shawl of mine isn't near warm enough for an evening the likes of this."

Uncle Zeke dipped his mustache in response, and off they went, holding hands, walking gingerly across the snow-covered cemetery grounds.

Once they were out of earshot, Mary turned and gave her sister a stern look. "I'm not spending the evening with that woman. Just drop me off at the house!"

"What should I tell her then?"

"Tell her we just buried our mother and I need some time alone. She'll understand. And if she doesn't, then it's just too bad."

"All right Mary, calm down, we'll drop you off. But please let me tell Aunt Gertrude that you're feeling ill effects from the day, that you have a headache, or the such. I don't want to be in the same house with her if she's miffed at you for choosing not to visit."

"Tell her I have a headache. Tell her if I'm feeling better I'll bundle up and walk on over to see you all later in the evening—but don't get her hopes up."

Darkness fell, lamps were lit, and Mary slipped into a night-gown. It occurred to Mary that she would be spending her first Christmas Eve alone. Wondering if she actually was starting to feel out of sorts, she brewed a pot of tea to warm herself up and calm herself down.

Mary was sipping from a teacup when she slowly pushed open the door to her mother's bedroom. Walking in, she lit an oil lamp, and stood for a moment at the foot of her mother's deathbed. Contemplating days past, Mary tried to recall happier times, but instead, an odd assortment of memories raced through her head.

When Mary and Becky were first adopted, they were thought to be identical twins, but as time passed it became obvious that they were not identical at all, just sisters who shared the same womb. Now in their mid-twenties, Becky was the pretty and outgoing one while Mary was plainer in appearance and introspective. Both, however, were blessed with flowing reddish hair and fair complexions.

When they were young girls, mother would tell them that God had marked Mary with a stubby pinky finger so that she could tell the two apart. But as Mary grew older, and found the shortened pinky finger to be more of a detriment than a divine blessing, she questioned if God or man had been responsible for such a deformed finger on an otherwise perfectly beautiful hand. Mother just shrugged the query off, as she did most all of Mary's questions having to do with her and her sister's first few years of life.

Mary and Becky shared a happy childhood. They did chores together, played together, and sought out their mother's warmth and understanding during difficult times. Becky grew up to be one of the prettiest young ladies in the neighborhood, sought by all the handsome, eligible bachelors. Robert, the town mayor's son, pursued the hardest and eventually won her hand in matrimony. Mary, an insatiable bookworm, became one of the first women to teach grammar school in Central Indiana. She was also a diligent caregiver for her aging mother.

Mary stared at the lid of the steamer trunk that sat at the foot of mother's bed. Becky and Mary had made a promise that they would wait until the weekend to sort through mother's personal belongings and legal papers. Part of the reason for this agreement was Becky's concern that Mary would seek out what she's always yearned to know—their birthparents' identities—and perhaps jump to incorrect conclusions or perhaps fall into despair, all without Becky at her side to comfort her. Becky, on the other hand, did not care who had given birth to them; she was raised by a loving mother, and that alone was sufficient for her peace of mind.

But Mary couldn't wait for her sister to join her. It was only Monday and the weekend seemed an eternity away. Besides, Becky had deserted her on the evening of their mother's funeral, as well as the eve of Christ's birthday. It was up to her to sort matters out, here and now, once and for all.

Mary pulled up a stool from a corner of the room, placed her empty tea cup on the floor, and attempted to yank open the trunk's lid. It was locked. A strange-shaped key, she remembered, was kept in the top drawer of mother's armoire. She rushed to fetch it.

The key fit and the lid swung open. Mary sat down, paused for a second as her heart pounded a bit louder, and began sorting through her adoption mother's earthly possessions.

It was, at first, a poignant but disappointing journey. Familiar items led the way, most of which brought back memories, some good and some not so good. The trunk's topmost layers were mostly articles of clothing and old blankets. Towards the bottom were stored books and various sundries, including a worn bible, sheets of church music, and some odd pieces of jewelry that Mary could never recall her mother ever wearing. She quickly worked her way down to the bottom of the trunk, but nothing of great interest was found; no will, no property deed, no birth certificates, and most disappointing to Mary, no adoption papers.

Surely mother would have kept these important documents somewhere in her bedroom. Mary looked around the tiny room for hiding places. Having cared for her mother these past few years, she was familiar with the contents of her armoire. Everything else mother owned was out in plain sight.

Mary thought that if this room has a secret hiding place, it must be a clever one, and best searched for in the light of day. Disappointed, she began reloading the trunk, starting with the old bible. Placing the bible down, Mary was struck by the hollow sound it made when the book came to rest at the bottom of the trunk. Perhaps this trunk has a false floor? She gently tapped on the floor of the trunk with the tips of her fingers, and yes, there was a resonance to the tapping sounds. Mary searched the trunk's exterior surfaces, but could not detect anything out of the ordinary. She then pulled it away from the foot of the bed and, sure enough, there appeared to be a concealed drawer in the backside of the trunk.

Flushed with excitement, Mary searched with her hands for a way in which to spring open the drawer, without success, until she pressed both hands firmly against it and jiggled it up and down, first softly, then a bit harder. A shallow compartment, containing legal documents, appeared before Mary's eyes.

Mary's hands began to shake. She arose from the floor, accidentally knocking over her empty teacup.

"All right, Mary," she said aloud to herself, "Keep it together. Stay calm!"

She carefully emptied the drawer's contents, sat back down on the stool, and began to read. The topmost document was the one she had sought after for as long as she could remember; words exploded off of the page:

> Natural Mother: Unknown
> Natural Father: Unknown
> Adoptive Mother: Gertrude Wilson
> Adoptive Father: Ezekiel Wilson
> Date of Adoption: December 29, 1864
> Location: Female Orphan Asylum, Savannah, Georgia

Dinner was served late. Gathered around the table were Aunt Gertrude and Uncle Zeke, Becky and Robert. Uncle Zeke sat at the head of the table and Robert sat opposite to him. An undisturbed place setting marked Mary's empty seat.

Table candles were lit, prayers of thanks were said, and a small roast goose was carved and served. Side dishes were set out on the table for passing. Only the foursome's somber clothing and subdued demeanor hinted that this was not a typical Christmas Eve gathering.

There was a knock on the door.

"That must be Mary now. She's feeling better; thank goodness, the poor girl. Zeke, don't just sit there, let Mary in. She must be freezing!"

Uncle Zeke rose from his seat of honor and opened the front door. In burst Mary, who gave Uncle Zeke a quick hug before quickly removing her coat, scarf, and knit hat.

"Sorry I'm late. I hope I haven't inconvenienced you, Aunt Gertrude. I drank a cup of hot tea and my head cleared up, and so here I am, after all. Mmm… dinner smells good."

Uncle Zeke smiled as he collected Mary's outerwear and walked them into a back room.

"We're so glad you could join us after all. Please sit right down, Mary," said Aunt Gertrude. "We just started serving dinner."

Becky's eyes followed Mary as she walked over and sat down at the table. Something must be up, she thought to herself.

Uncle Zeke returned to the table and everyone turned their attentions to Christmas Eve dinner, with the exception of Becky, who tried to catch Mary's attention by furtively glancing at her with a quizzical expression on her face. Mary was too wound up to notice her sister.

Unlike past Christmas Eve dinners, discussions were sporadic and subdued. The ticking of a mantle clock filled in voids in conversation. Eventually, stomachs were filled and clanking silverware came to a standstill.

"It's a shame you girls never met your father!" Aunt Gertrude exclaimed.

"He was a fine gentleman. A God-fearing man, he was!"

Father had succumbed to smallpox during an epidemic that ravaged Central Indiana back in the winter of 1865.

"Did my sister ever show you his bible?"

Becky looked at Mary while shaking her head no. Mary raised her eyebrows and gently nodded her head yes.

"Well I've never seen anything like it—I can say in all sincerity. He wrote all over that bible, filling in margins with notes and even little sketches. Isaac should have been a minister, I'd always say! I used to say that to Beatrice. Your father could have preached scripture with insight that nobody else ever thought of."

"It's so nice of you to say that," said Becky.

"You girls were properly raised by a fine, devout Christian woman. You know you were. My sister was all of that—she certainly was. You were very fortunate to be adopted by my sister Beatrice. Without a husband, she raised two little angels, and now you've grown up to be refined and beautiful young ladies. We are so proud of you both."

Becky smiled and replied, "Thank you, Aunt Gertrude! That's very sweet of you to say so."

Mary, feeling she was about to burst, had to say something; but it would be something quite different from the conversation at hand.

"We are very fortunate, Aunt Gertrude! We were so blessed to have been adopted—not once, but twice."

Everyone at the table froze and all eyes turned towards Aunt Gertrude. A pained look came across Becky's face; she now understood why Mary was acting so strangely. Becky's worst fears had come to pass.

Aunt Gertrude was at a loss for words, an event hardly ever before witnessed.

"What... what, on heaven's earth, are you speaking of, dear child?"

"Along with father's bible I found two sets of adoption papers. I'm sure you're aware of all this, Aunt Gertrude. Your signature is on one of them."

It was as if a lightning bolt had struck Aunt Gertrude. Becky also felt a jolt from Mary's surprise announcement.

"Sweetie, you don't understand, there was only one adoption. You and your sister were in the Jeffersonville Orphan Asylum when your mother and father first laid eyes on you. Didn't your mother ever tell you this story?"

Mary ignored her aunt and turned towards Uncle Zeke.

"Uncle Zeke, during the war, were you ever stationed in Savannah, Georgia?"

Uncle Zeke went into sensory overload. He mumbled incoherently, gently placed both hands on the table, slowly rose from his seat, and walked into a back room of the house, closing the door behind him.

There was a moment of stunned silence.

"Now see what you've done, Mary. You know how upset Uncle Zeke gets when he's asked about the war. That poor man was traumatized by that awful war. Please, apologize to him—and no more of this kind of talk, especially tonight."

"I'll apologize to Uncle Zeke," Mary said contritely, "but I believe there is a great deal of explaining to be done. Mother never talked with us about our adoption, but she left behind papers that show that Becky and I were adopted not once, but twice. The first time was in Savannah by you and Uncle Zeke, and the second time was in Jeffersonville by mother and father—except according to father's death certificate, he was actually deceased at the time of that adoption. So, as you can see, I'm a bit confused!"

Becky let out a faint gasp.

"Mary, are you positive about all this?" asked Becky. She was so upset, her voice was cracking. Robert placed his hand on his wife's back in an attempt to comfort her.

"The documents are quite clear. If you'd like to see them, they're in my coat pocket. And Becky, the sad part is, our birth parents are listed as unknown."

"I'm so sorry," whispered Becky. Becky understood what a bitter disappointment this was to her sister.

Aunt Gertrude sensed a thorny problem in the making and she decided to head it off at the pass.

"Mary, you were always obsessed with understanding the details surrounding your adoption. These papers you found are just legal documents, legal gibberish that can easily be misinterpreted. They're not important. What is important to understand is that your mother loved you girls with all of her heart, and…"

Aunt Gertrude began to choke up.

"…and you girls gave her reason to live, to carry on, after the war, and after that smallpox epidemic took so many of us, including your dear father."

Mary sat motionless, stunned by this last remark.

"Aunt Gertrude, I owe both you and Uncle Zeke an apology," Mary replied softly.

Just then, the door to the back room swung open and Uncle Zeke slowly walked into the dining room. He was wearing his old army uniform and holding a kepi hat in his hand. The uniform fit quite well, and Uncle Zeke looked every bit the dashing Federal infantry sergeant he had been a quarter of a century ago.

"Oh my goodness," Aunt Gertrude yelled out as she pushed her seat back and stood up. "Zeke, what on earth are you doing! Take that uniform off right now! Have you gone completely mad?"

"No, Gertrude, it's time. They need to know."

"Know what? What are you babbling about?"

"Beatrice could have destroyed those adoption papers but she didn't. She left them behind for a reason. Our nieces need to know their story—the real story—from beginning to end!"

Aunt Gertrude sat back down and hung her head in her hands. The genie was out of the bottle.

Uncle Zeke sat down at the head of the table, placed his old kepi hat down in front of him, drew a deep breath and said, "It's my turn to say some things."

Uncle Zeke appeared calm and focused, as if he had prepared for this moment his entire life.

"People said that we were animals—that we pillaged and set fire to everything and anything in our path. I know many of our soldiers were out of control, but most of us just did what we were ordered to do—nothing more, nothing less. Railroads, crops, cotton mills, factories—that's what we were sent down south to destroy. And we went about it like disciplined soldiers, which we, for the most part, were. But many a time we were ordered to conduct heinous acts. We stole food and valuables from people's homes. We burned down the homes of a lot of good people—the homes of women who had lost their husbands to the war and were struggling to raise small children. And for this I'll never forgive myself, till my dying day."

Uncle Zeke paused to collect himself. His tiny audience, including Aunt Gertrude, sat and stared, hanging on his every word.

"General Sherman was convinced that his army could move through Georgia, without supply lines, by living off the fat of the land. Each day we sent out companies to search for food. The Union army called them foraging parties, but the Southerners, they called 'em bummers. I'm still not exactly sure what it means to be a bummer, but it doesn't sound like they were complimenting us any. Soon we attracted a ragtag bunch of civilian bummers—they followed our army, picking the countryside clean of whatever food and valuables we left behind. Those poor Southerners were pillaged, coming and going. They never had a chance."

"I was older than nearly all of the enlisted men and most of my officers too, so maybe I just saw things differently than the rest of them. I didn't want to do a lot of what they ordered me to do, but I had to. Treason was punishable by firing squad. Many an officer would order his men to 'court martial this traitor and then shoot him.' And just like that, you were branded a traitor and executed—it was that easy."

"We were attached to General Sherman's southern wing, under the command of General Howard, and we were marching through such poor countryside that there was hardly anything worth putting a torch to. Most people down there were dressed in rags and bone thin from lack of good food."

"One morning, our captain ordered the company to proceed about three miles down a railroad spur and set fire to a coaling station. We were anxious to get down there and carry out this order, as we were wondering what kind of spectacular fire a big old pile of coal would make."

"We started out, and, as usual, we're three miles down the track and we can't find the coaling station. It seemed like everything we were ordered to do back then was twice as hard as the officers made it out to be. Well, we marched about two miles further and we spotted this small, single-dock loading station—an old wooden structure. It was low on coal, but, nevertheless, we all felt it would still make a spectacular fire."

"Without hesitating, we surrounded the tower and lit some torches. We were instructed to throw the torches directly onto the coal pile, which we did. And that's when all hell broke loose."

Chapter 2

Central Georgia, November, 1864

"It ain't burning at all!" Corporal Samuel Hartsdale exclaimed to no one in particular. "Must be wet coal in there!"

"Give 'er a minute," replied Sergeant Ezekiel Wilson. "She'll start burning after the water steams out."

"I heared' somebody in there," yelled Private Henry Diggs, on the run from the far side of the tower and heading directly towards Sergeant Wilson.

"You hear people in there?" asked Sergeant Wilson.

"Sounds like babies crying! I swear it does! Come over to the other side and you'll hear it, plain as day!"

Sergeant Wilson didn't waste time listening for babies' cries. He ran to the far end of the tower and dashed up the stairway leading into the structure. Seeing no signs of life in the obvious places, he tried looking down onto the coal pile, but rising smoke and steam prevented him from keeping his eyes open. He thought he heard the wailing of not one but a couple of babies. He could distinctly hear one of them crying out "Mammy, Mammy."

Sergeant Wilson looked behind him and realized that Corporal Hartsdale and Private Diggs had followed him into the tower and were standing behind him.

"I'm going down onto the coal pile," yelled Sergeant Wilson, "I think they're right below us."

"Git near the edge and give me yer' arms and we'll help lower ya' down," Private Diggs replied. "Wave yer' hands over yer' head when ya' need us to pull ya' up again," he added.

They lowered Sergeant Wilson down onto the surface of the coal pile and he disappeared beneath a sea of smoke and steam. Seconds later, his raised arms emerged from the haze clutching a grimy baby garbed in a cutoff burlap bag. Private Diggs snatched the baby, which was alive and kicking. Arms emerged again; this time a similar looking, but lifeless baby was offered up.

Two outstretched arms emerged from the haze and Corporal Hartsdale and Private Diggs each grabbed one and together they yanked their sergeant back up to safety. Sergeant Wilson went down to all fours, coughing and choking, trying to catch his breath.

Attention turned to the tiny babies dressed in burlap sacks.

"I'm OK! Grab 'em!" yelled Sergeant Wilson, "Let's git' the hell out of here!"

Outside the coaling station the entire company of thirty soldiers looked on at a safe distance. Steam and smoke could be seen pouring out of every crevice of the old wooden structure.

The three rescuers carefully made their way down the stairway. Sergeant Wilson was unsteady and coughing uncontrollably. Private Diggs descended holding a wailing baby. Corporal Hartsdale was concerned because his baby wasn't moving at all.

"There better be gold in those gunny sacks," yelled out Captain Baker, who ran up to meet them at the base of the stairway; he had not yet figured out what all the fuss was about.

Sergeant Wilson collapsed to the ground, coughing, still trying to clear his lungs. Two soldiers rushed over and dragged him clear of the smoldering tower. Corporal Hartsdale and Private Diggs ran to safety.

Corporal Hartsdale knelt down to one knee and cradled the lifeless baby in his arms. Fresh air was a miracle elixir; the baby began to kick and cry.

"Thank the Lord," he exclaimed.

It was obvious they had found twins, perhaps Caucasian, but that was difficult to tell for sure due to coal soot. They were emaciated from lack of food, and their raggedy diapers were obviously, and understandably, soiled.

"Well I'll be!" exclaimed Captain Baker, "What kind of mother would abandon her little babies on a coal pile? Now I've seen it all!"

Other soldiers moved in closer to witness an unusual sight: Private Diggs and Corporal Hartsdale cradling these babies as if they were their own children.

"Sergeant Wilson was the brave one!" exclaimed Private Diggs, "He jumped onto that burning coal pile and rescued 'em both."

The captain turned towards Sergeant Wilson, who was sitting on the ground, just now starting to breathe normally.

"That's one fine piece of humanity you just displayed in there, Sergeant, you risking your life for those little babies."

"Thank you, captain. I'm not sure what came over me."

Captain Baker was a tall, imposing figure of a man. He had been employed as a railroad engineer prior to the war, and was commissioned a lieutenant when mustered into service. He proved to be a strong-willed, profanity-laced leader of men. Compliments to his men were rare, and as such, much appreciated.

"But now we've got to find these babies a place to stay. That ain't going to be easy in this God-forsaken place!"

"Yes sir."

The old coaling station finally succumbed. It burst into flames and the heat emitted was intense. Soldiers stared at it, mesmerized by the sight, even as they were driven back by a wave of hot air.

"We're moving out! Form up, on the quick!" yelled Captain Baker.

The twins made the company's march back to camp an unusual one. Biscuits soaked in canteen water nourished them and dampened rags were used to clean off the layer of soot and grim that covered their faces. A linen undershirt, donated by the captain himself, was torn in half and fashioned into two somewhat functional baby diapers. The three rescuers took turns holding the tiny girls, who, for most of the journey, quietly stared at their newly found friends.

How the babies came to be left at the coaling station became a matter of great debate. One theory had their mother pilfering coal when she saw Union soldiers approaching. Panic set in, and she decided to hide inside the tower with her babies rather than surrender. If this were the case, than an ill-advised decision cost the twins' mother her life.

None of the soldiers could believe that a mother would run away from the coaling station, leaving her two babies behind to fend for themselves. This was too callous an act, even for the strange inhabitants of this poor, war-torn countryside.

Everyone in the company had an opinion about the twins' age. Many guessed a year old, while a few others, taking into account poor diet, speculated as high as two years old. All in all, one year of age was the consensus.

After an hour's march the company paused at the first village they came upon. A heavy, black plume from the burning coaling station could still be seen on the horizon.

It was not much of a village, just a dozen or so shacks along a bend in a stream, only a stone's throw from the railroad tracks. Captain Baker, anxious to get rid of the babies, knocked on several doors, but, understandably, nobody came out to greet him. Finally he spotted a young lady hanging laundry out to dry on a backyard clothesline. When she saw him walking towards her, she was startled, and became fearful.

"You know of any twin girls, about one or two years of age, with reddish hair?"

"No sir, I sure do not." When she spoke, a missing front tooth belied her otherwise soft, youthful appearance.

"No family around here has twin girls? We don't mean you any harm. We just want to get these babies back together with their mother."

"No, I don't know of any twin girls at all in these here parts."

"Well we found them wandering around alone out there, and we request that you take them off our hands."

"I'd sure like to oblige, but I've got three children of my own, and we don't have nearly enough food to eat. I'm sorry. I can't be taking in no war orphans."

"Is there anyone else you know of around here who could take care of them? If we can't leave them with somebody here then we'll just have to toss 'em into a river!"

The lady's eyes grew large and she started to shake with fear.

"No, Mr. Officer, we are all poor folks here, and I…, I…"

Captain Baker realized he had overplayed his hand.

"Please ma'm, don't worry, we wouldn't be throwing any babies into rivers. I apologize for that ungentlemanly remark. We just need to find them a place to stay. It's dangerous for babies to be traveling with an army."

Greatly relieved, she let out a sigh, gave the captain a weak nod, and started to say "There's a good-sized town about three miles south of here them Yankees ain't burned down yet…" but she stopped midsentence, realizing that what she was saying might offend the officer. Her eyes grew wide and fearful again.

"Thanks for the information. I'll leave you to your chores. And ma'm, before we head out I'll have one of my men stop by with some flour and molasses for you and the children."

"Thank you, Mr. Officer. Thank you so much!"

Camp broke in the morning and General Howard's wing was on the move again, heading east, towards Savannah, Georgia.

Sherman's army was averaging a dozen miles a day, and there would be no letup until the Atlantic Ocean was in sight.

Some late night bartering with a group of civilian bummers resulted in baby diapers and two tiny dresses for the twins. At dawn, Corporal Hartsdale and Private Diggs gave them a bath, dressed them in proper clothes, and combed their fine red hair. Every soldier who saw the twins that morning gave the girls a big hello and offered to share their breakfast rations with them. The twins were quick to win the hearts of most soldiers in Captain Baker's company. Of course, there were a few men who grumbled about an army at war turning into "nothin' more then a bunch of babysitters."

General Howard's wing quick-stepped their way across the Deep South, pausing to destroy infrastructure of value to the Southern cause; and yes, many, many private homes were also put to the torch. When on the move, the twins were either held by one of their rescuers or they rode in a supply wagon towards the rear of the column. Most nights they slept in Corporal Hartsdale's tent while the corporal hunkered down near the tent's open front flap.

The regiment's medical doctor examined the twins and the girls were given a clean bill of health except for what appeared to be a bad case of diaper rash. After the exam the three rescuers argued over the proper interval for changing diapers and settled on three changes per day: morning, noontime, and nighttime.

"No matter what, rain or shine, them diapers have to be changed!" ordered Sergeant Wilson.

The twins weren't smiling very much, but their appetites were good. They gobbled up hot meals faster than the men, much to everyone's entertainment. A large circle of soldiers began to look out for the twins' general welfare. Captain Baker's company found creative ways to clothe and care for them, although the efficiency of their efforts was questionable. After a week on the march, Sergeant Wilson had to chide his fellow soldiers for accumulating too many dresses and nary a sun hat. A week later the sergeant had to complain to them again, this time for the exorbitant number of rag dolls and wooden toys the girls had been given.

Caring for the twins had a transforming effect on the battlefield conduct of Captain Baker's company. Many began to seek out and protect the homes of mothers with small children. If the mother of the house became fearful for her family's safety, a soldier would stand guard at her front door until the wave of blue-clad soldiers passed through town. Several soldiers donated food, sometimes their only rations for the day, to households with small children. On one occasion the lady of the house invited a young private into her kitchen so they could all share his generous gift of biscuits, salt pork, and coffee.

Milk was an issue. To buy or confiscate fresh milk for the twins was to take it out of the mouths of starving Southern children. The soldiers of Captain Baker's company decided to be very generous to local farmers when bartering for fresh milk. But if a farmer wasn't forthright with them, they would confiscate the milk and distribute it among families with small children. Of course the twins always received more than their fair share of this booty.

One evening after supper, while sitting around a campfire, the rescuers had a spirited debate over what names should be given to the twins. As everyone had a difficult time telling the two apart, Corporal Hartsdale argued that naming them would be a futile exercise. But Sergeant Wilson and Private Diggs insisted, repeating over and over again that "these girls need good, Christian names." Thus the twins came to be known as Mary and Rebecca; Mary after the sergeant's grandmother, and Rebecca after the private's girlfriend back home. But Corporal Hartsdale was proven correct, as the impromptu naming ceremony did not at all clarify matters. After their next bath together, nobody could figure out which girl was Mary and which girl was Rebecca.

Sergeant Wilson knocked on the front door. "I know some-one's in there. Come to the door!" he yelled out.

The door half opened. A young lady with two small children in tow meekly asked "What do you want from us?"

"We're not here to cause any damage or to pilfer anything belonging to you, ma'm. I'm just in need of advice, if you could spare a few minutes of your time."

"You want advice? I haven't seen any armies pass by, and if I did, do ya' think I'd tell ya'?"

"No ma'm, I'm not asking you to spy for us. I just need to know… well, what I really need to know is… could you tell me… what's a good remedy for diaper rash?"

The lady stared at the sergeant with a quizzical look on her face, then slammed the door closed and bolted it shut.

Chapter 3

Low Country, December, 1864

When Captain Baker's company first entered into the swampland that straddles the border of South Carolina and Georgia, they realized that their march through Central Georgia had been nothing more than a stroll in the park. The Savannah River's marshy flood plains proved difficult to move an army through, and the few plantations they came upon had already been picked clean by Union and Confederate cavalry raiders. Bummers who were not Union soldiers stayed back in the farmlands of Central Georgia, while army bummers found little of value to pilfer. Supply wagons had trouble negotiating the swamp's poor roads, and so rations ran low; soldiers went for days without decent food, sometimes relying on a biscuit or a handful of rice to ward off hunger pains.

Making matters worse, there were rumors of marauding rebel cavalry in the area. Foot soldiers don't fear fighting horse soldiers on an open field of battle, but stealth cavalry attacks on infantry encampments are quite a different matter. After a difficult march and scant food for supper, many soldiers slept uneasily at night, with loaded guns at their sides.

The twins were immune to these hardships, thanks to the caring soldiers of Captain Baker's company. A handful of corn became a fried mush cake for breakfast, while rice would be boiled to a pasty consistency and fed to the girls as soup for late night supper. Although the food wasn't as nutritious as it had been, there certainly was no drop-off in quantity.

The twins began to warm up to army life. The three rescuers became their adopted family and several others of the company became extended family members. At night, the girls usually drifted off to sleep in someone's arms. They woke up each morning in their own tent with Corporal Hartsdale lying outside, blocking the opened tent flap, snoring away. A little game they played at daybreak was to crawl onto Corporal Hartsdale and poke at him until he woke up, at which point he would pretend to chide them for so rudely disturbing him.

And yes, the twins were finally smiling. But this was about to change.

Captain Baker's company had been marching through Low Country for two weeks, and his men were worn down and hungry. Troublesome to all was a confirmed skirmish between Union and Confederate cavalry, just a dozen miles southwest of their position. Sergeant Wilson warned anyone who would listen: "It's just a matter of time."

That night they set up camp in a clearing near the intersection of two well-trodden dirt roads. Of the ten companies in their brigade, they were positioned on the southernmost flank that night. Their isolation from most of the brigade and the vulnerability of the campsite gave Captain Baker and his men cause for concern. Extra pickets were posted, and the men slept uneasily, cradling their loaded Springfield rifles. Night passed without incident.

At sunup, thirty hungry soldiers gulped down a cold breakfast, began breaking down camp, and prepared to resume their march towards the Confederate-occupied city of Savannah, Georgia. This plan was interrupted when Rebel raiders appeared, out of nowhere, striking with deadly force.

With little warning Confederate horsemen stampeded through the partially broken campsite, firing carbines and swinging sabers. Union soldiers scattered in every direction. Captain Baker, clad in trousers, suspenders and undershirt, stood bravely at the center of a deadly swirl of blue and butternut, holding his sword high in the air and barking out orders that none could hear owing to the noise and chaos. Many of the company grabbed their rifles and managed to squeeze off a shot before turning and running for cover. Several soldiers were shot in the back, while others had to fend off slashing saber attacks. As a last resort, many of Baker's men fell flat to the ground, hoping to avoid the lead storm above them. Although it lasted but a few minutes, the loss of life and injuries sustained was severe.

And just like that, the rebels galloped off, riding through the dirt road intersection and melting back into the murky landscape.

"Assemble men, on the quick, with your weapons!" yelled out Captain Baker. This was the first of the captain's commands that morning that could be heard by his company.

"Form up here!" he yelled out as he pointed to the center of the campsite with his sword. The men quickly assembled in front of Captain Baker.

A picket came running down the road yelling "They're gone! They're gone!" He then stopped dead in his tracks, pointed and hollered out: "Watch out, here comes our boys!"

Union cavalry thundered past the campsite, in hot pursuit of the enemy. They galloped through the intersection and disappeared down the same dirt road taken by rebel horsemen just minutes prior. The sound of clumping and clanking gradually became more distant.

And then the swamp became eerily quiet.

Of the thirty men in Captain Baker's company, twenty-two answered roll call. The captain's heart sank. Three blue-clad bodies were discovered behind a fallen tree, their weapons close by, while two butternut-clad soldiers lay lifeless in a clearing directly in front of them. These brave Union soldiers had kept their wits about them, took cover, and began firing and reloading as fast as they could. Their reward was deadly revenge, meted out by carbine and sword.

Sergeant Wilson found Private Diggs and asked him, "Have you seen Corporal Hartsdale? Where the hell are the girls?" Private Diggs shook his head no in response to both queries. They set out together, first searching through the remnants of the campsite, then walking along the surrounding tree line.

It was a sight that brought tears to their eyes. What had just happened was clear; Corporal Hartsdale had snatched up the twins and was running for cover when he was shot through the back. The minié ball passed through his upper body, exited his chest, and in so doing blew away the tip of one of Mary's little fingers.

Rebecca was found crawling on Corporal Hartsdale's lifeless body, trying to wake him up, as the girls had done each morning for the past several weeks. A blood-splattered Mary was sitting up, leaning against Corporal Hartsdale's body, in a state of shock, her missing finger tip bleeding profusely.

"God Almighty," exclaimed Sergeant Wilson, as he bent down and snatched up Mary. He began squeezing the tiny stub of her bleeding finger, much to Mary's dismay.

Private Diggs picked up Rebecca, hugged her and tried to console her. "Now, now little one, it'll be alright," he said in a soothing voice, as his mother used to say to him when he was just a child.

Armies on the move need to move quickly and efficiently. The wounded were sent by wagon to the nearest field hospital. Corporal Hartsdale was buried in a hastily dug, shallow grave, marked by a crudely fashioned wooden cross; alongside him were the graves of his three fallen comrades in arms.

Nearby, separate from the four Union graves, were the graves of two more brave American soldiers.

It is the mark of cowardice for a soldier to be shot in the back during battle. Sergeant Wilson thought about this, and also the possibility that Corporal Hartsdale's body might eventually be exhumed and re-interred at a nearby cemetery, as so often is the case. And so with this in mind, he wrote a simple note and placed it with Corporal Hartsdale's body:

> Here lies Corporal Samuel Hartsdale, a good Christian man, who was shot and killed while bravely protecting two baby girls who didn't belong on a field of battle, on this day, December 15, 1864.
>
> Sergeant Ezekiel Wilson, 83rd
Regiment, Company E, Army of the Tennessee

Four dead and eight injured, Captain Baker's official report read. But everyone knew there were nine injuries sustained that morning, and they swore to one another that nobody would ever again harm their little babies.

Chapter 4

Savannah, Georgia, December, 1864

General Sherman's three-hundred-mile march through the heart of the Deep South culminated with the bloodless capture of Savannah, Georgia. The city was abandoned by occupying Confederate forces just hours ahead of the advancing Union army.

Captain Baker's company entered Savannah on Friday evening, the 23rd of December, and set up camp in an isolated field on the outskirts of the city. All were happy to have seen the last of the swamp lands of Low Country, but painful memories of its hardships and tragedies lingered.

The twins fell into a fit of melancholy once again, which was understandable considering all that they had just endured. The loss of Corporal Hartsdale, who had taken on more than his fair share of caring for the girls, was a cruel blow to them.

While back in Low Country, the regiment's medical officer had treated Mary's wounded pinkie finger. He carefully instructed Sergeant Wilson and Private Diggs on how to clean and care for the wound. So both men were pleased when they brought Mary to see an army surgeon in Savannah and he told them he was satisfied with the wound's appearance. But the surgeon, a major by rank, also gave them a not-so-thinly-disguised warning.

"These babies need to be cared for in a proper home, and kept out of harm's way. So I must ask you two, what are your intentions? What are you planning to do with these babies?"

"Well sir," replied Sergeant Wilson, "what we planned on doing was finding a home for them here in Savannah."

"That will not be easy, Sergeant. Wealthy folks in this city resent us—they wouldn't give a Union soldier the correct time of day. And the rest of the population is struggling to feed their own families."

"Yes, sir. We understand."

"By the way, who else in your company knows about these babies, besides you two men?"

"Everybody in the company knows, from Captain Baker on down."

"I'll ignore that comment. We need to keep Captain Baker and the rest of the company clear of this mess. From now on, only the two of you know anything about the existence of these babies. Is that clear?"

"Yes, sir!" replied both Sergeant Wilson and Private Diggs.

"I'm going to pass word on up to headquarters that this situation exists and that it will be resolved within a week. You either find a home for these babies, or you'll leave them at a local orphanage. You have until Friday of next week to get this done. Is what I'm saying perfectly clear?"

"Yes, sir." replied Sergeant Wilson, in a weak voice. The doctor could tell that they were not at all pleased with this unexpected turn of events.

"Now get out of here and start looking for a home for these babies. They deserve better than getting shot up on the battlefield. It's our job to fight the rebels, not theirs."

"Understood, sir."

"You have until Friday of next week to get this done. You're dismissed!"

Sergeant Wilson and Private Diggs were disheartened by the doctor's ultimatum. They had hoped that a healthy dose of peaceful city life would prove amenable to the twins; maybe even get them to start smiling again. They also needed the luxury of time to find a decent family that would be willing to take the twins in. Now the sword of Damocles hung over their heads.

"Maybe the orphanages around here ain't so bad," suggested Private Diggs, as they slowly walked back to camp with Mary sound asleep in Sergeant Wilson's arms. "Maybe we should go take a look at 'em and see what kinda' places they are."

"Maybe we should. Or maybe we need to take matters into our own hands."

Later that day Sergeant Wilson and Private Diggs walked over to the Female Orphan Asylum of Savannah. They found conditions there deplorable. The wards were overcrowded, the children were dressed in tattered clothes, and everyone, including the staff, appeared underfed and unhappy. They agreed that placing the twins in an orphanage was not an option.

Frustration and despair set in as word of the doctor's ultimatum spread among the men of Captain Baker's company.

The Great War, the doctor's harsh ultimatum, and all of life's uncertainties were placed on hold; it was Christmas Eve.

The twins were joined in their melancholy by just about every soldier in General Sherman's army, except perhaps General William Tecumseh Sherman himself, who offered seasonal greetings to his commander-in-chief, President Abraham Lincoln, in a hastily written telegraph message:

> "I beg to present to you as a Christmas gift, the city of Savannah, with one hundred and fifty heavy guns and plenty of ammunition, also about 25,000 bales of cotton."

To which President Lincoln promptly responded:

> "Many, many thanks for your Christmas gift, the capture of Savannah. When you were about leaving Atlanta for the Atlantic coast, I was anxious, if not fearful; but feeling that you were the better judge, and remembering that 'nothing risked, nothing gained,' I did not interfere. Now, the undertaking being a success, the honor is yours."

Chapter 5

Savannah, Christmas Day, 1864

A soaking rain passed over the campsite early that Christmas morning. Private Diggs, who took over most of Corporal Hartsdale's childcare duties, bedded down inside the twin's tent. Except for those soldiers on picket duty, the entire company slept late, a luxury no one could recall enjoying since they marched off to fight this never-ending war.

By word of mouth, the soldiers heard about the availability of fresh oysters, and so a company wagon was dispatched to the Savannah River to investigate this possibility. The thought of roasted oysters for Christmas dinner had the men salivating in anticipation. Indiana boys who had never tasted a shellfish in their lives were dreaming of roasted oysters.

Later that morning the rain let up and the melodious sound of distant church bells wafted over the campsite. Sergeant Wilson and Private Diggs dressed the twins in their fanciest dresses and they all set off to find a Christmas service. Walking towards the sound of church bells, the foursome stumbled upon a large, impressive-looking church, built of stone and adorned with elaborate stained glass windows.

They were walking up the church's front steps when an elderly parishioner intercepted them.

"Listen, gentlemen, I don't mean to cause any trouble, but it may not be a good idea for you all to join our congregation in worship today. There are a lot of bitter people in there that resent your occupation of our city. Most of the women have husbands off fightin' the war. Some had their husbands chased out of town when you boys marched in. We also have a couple of war widows in there. So I hope you understand. I'm not sure how they'll react if you all go inside with your blue uniforms on."

"We don't want to disrupt your Christmas service," responded Sergeant Wilson, "but we are Christians in need of a Christian church. Do you know where we can find one?" Sergeant Wilson held just the right balance of inquisitiveness and sarcasm in his voice.

"You'll see several churches just down the road, a bit further, not far at all. Most denominations are represented. I have to say that you and the little ladies look like good, decent folk, and I hope you can find a place to worship today. But it's just, as an occupying army, you're going to have a rough go of it, if you know what I mean."

"Thank you for the advice."

As they walked further down the road, Private Diggs sniffed loudly and said, "And they calls' themselves Christians!" Sergeant Wilson nodded his head in response.

The next church they came upon was a small, white-washed wooden structure, surrounded by well-dressed worshipers waiting patiently to enter the church's front door. As they neared the church, all eyes turned towards them, and there began much whispering back and forth. The crowd also stopped moving forward towards the front door of the church, and by so doing, entry into the church was blocked.

"Let's pass on this one," suggested Private Diggs.

"I agree—let's keep walking!"

And so they continued on. After passing by the church, Private Diggs looked back, smiled, and tipped his kepi hat, giving these Christmas morning worshipers something more to whisper about.

The next church they passed was boarded up and abandoned. Soon the well-kept city street took on more the appearance of a country road. They had been walking for just under an hour. The twins had fallen asleep in their arms.

And then they began to hear singing—strange singing, unlike any of the church hymns they grew up with.

They came upon a large church with a tall steeple that had more the appearance of a watch tower than a traditional church steeple. A painted sign over the opened front doors read *First African Baptist Church.*

They stopped, took it all in, and then stared blankly at each other.

"Should we try?" asked Private Diggs.

The singing came to a ragged halt and a small group of people exited the church and hurried down the front steps. An elderly bespectacled minister and several members of his congregation surrounded the foursome, greeting them with smiling faces.

"Welcome to our church!" the minister said. "We are just about to start Christmas services. I hope you gentlemen, and these fine young ladies, will be able to join us in worship today!"

The twins awoke from their brief naps. Their tiny heads pivoted around here and there, gazing bleary-eyed at the commotion taking place around them.

"We assumed that you were in the middle of services. We heard singing, so we didn't want to disturb you," replied Sergeant Wilson.

"That's not a problem—we were just warming up our voices! Come inside—worship with us today. This is a special Christmas for our congregation. You are welcome to join us!"

"Thank you."

The church was packed to capacity. The well-dressed folk were sitting towards the front, while the back pews appeared to be reserved for poorer members of the congregation, perhaps newly freed slaves. All eyes followed as the minister walked his guests down the center aisle. He seated them in the very first pew, closest to the tabernacle. Several people slid over and a few others took seats towards the rear of the church, so as to clear out this position of honor. Once everyone was reseated, the minister formally introduced their guests of honor.

"We have, joining us in worship today, two of our city's liberators, accompanied by two charming young ladies."

The congregation shouted out in unison: "Hallelujah!"

The minister then prompted his congregation to resume from where they had left off.

They sang and clapped to a stirring rendition of "Down by the Riverside" and followed this up with a softer, spiritual version of "Go Tell It on the Mountain." The twins looked around in wonderment; little Rebecca began clapping. Mary tried to imitate her sister, but the bandage wrapped around her injured finger made it difficult. This was the first time the rescuers had seen the girls clap their hands, and they could not help but let out broad smiles.

Seated next to them was a young, heavyset lady who kept glancing over at the twins; the girls reciprocated by staring at her and reaching their hands out towards her. Eventually both girls were sitting in her lap, a lap so wide that several more babies could have joined in without threat of overcrowding.

The church service was unlike anything Sergeant Wilson and Private Diggs had ever before experienced. After the congregation sang a few gospel songs, the minister stepped up to the pulpit and delivered an hour-long sermon. As the congregation settled in and the minister's soothing voice filled the church, the twins drifted off to sleep again, this time in the lap of their newfound friend.

The minister started off his sermon from the Book of Isaiah:

> "Seek the Lord while he may be found; call on him while he is near. Let the wicked forsake his way and the evil man his thoughts. Let him turn to the Lord,

and he will have mercy on him, and to our God, for he will freely pardon."

He then moved on to the Book of Joshua:

"When the trumpets sounded, the army shouted, and at the sound of the trumpet, when the men gave a loud shout, the wall collapsed, so everyone charged straight in, and they took the city. They devoted the city to the Lord."

Finally, he told the Christmas story from the Book of Matthew:

"After they had heard the king, they went on their way, and the star they had seen in the east went ahead of them until it stopped over the place where the child was. When they saw the star, they were overjoyed. On coming to the house, they saw the child with his mother Mary, and they bowed down and worshiped him. Then they opened their treasures and presented him with gifts of gold and of incense and of myrrh."

When the sermon ended, the congregation sang traditional Christmas songs. Lastly, all rose from their seats and, to the amazement of Sergeant Wilson and Private Diggs, they sang a stirring rendition of the popular pro-Union song "Battle Hymn of the Republic." The twins woke up; and they smiled.

⚬⚬⚬

When seated in a position of honor nearest the tabernacle, you are then last to exit the church. The minister greeted his four guests at the bottom of the church's front steps. It had just begun to softly rain.

"Thank you for worshiping with us today. I hope you enjoyed our Christmas service," the minister said, while shaking Sergeant Wilson's hand.

"We sure did, sir," Sergeant Wilson responded.

"Please, call me John—John Pease is my name."

"It's a pleasure to meet you, Reverend Pease. I'm Ezekiel Wilson, this here is Henry Diggs, and the young ladies' names are Rebecca and Mary."

"And so how is it that a couple of soldiers are so honored to be in the company of two such fine young ladies on a Christmas morning?"

"Well, it's a long story, sir... I'm sorry, I meant Reverend Pease. We found these girls in a tough situation back in Georgia, without their mother, and nobody there would take them in, so we've been caring for them ever since."

"They travelled with your army, through Georgia, all the way here?" asked an amazed Reverend Pease.

"Yes. It was an unusual journey for all of us."

"Now I'm curious, you never did meet their mother, am I correct?"

"Yes, that's right."

"So how then did they come about receiving their given names?"

"Why, we named them!" replied Private Diggs with a big smile on his face.

"When you had the girls baptized?" asked the reverend.

Private Diggs looked at Sergeant Wilson; they stared at each other for a moment.

"Well, no, I guess we just assumed that they had already been baptized," responded Sergeant Wilson. "Honestly, we never thought at all about getting them christened. Perhaps we should have."

"That's understandable—you two have a lot on your minds. Now this is strictly up to you, but tomorrow we have baptism services for all of our new members, and if you'd like to join us, I could christen these young ladies."

Sergeant Wilson and Private Diggs stared at each other again, for just an instant.

"We really appreciate your offer, Reverend Pease," replied Sergeant Wilson, "and if we can break free, we might be able take you up on it."

"Fine, then! Hopefully we'll see you all here tomorrow morning. We'll begin at nine o'clock."

The oysters were fresh and tasty, as advertised, and a non-traditional Christmas dinner was enjoyed by all the men of Captain Baker's company. They also received an unexpected Christmas present from General Sherman. His army drew pay for the first time since early September.

Chapter 6

Savannah, Monday

And so it came to be that Mary and Rebecca were baptized into the Christian faith. It may have been their second time around, but of this possibility no one really knew for sure.

The baptism ceremony, by triple immersion in the church's stone baptismal font, was a traumatic event for the twins, and afterwards they wailed uncontrollably. The girls could not be consoled until the heavyset lady from yesterday's Christmas service asked if she could hold them again. She cradled them in her arms and gently rocked them off to sleep.

"I must say that lady has a way with Mary and Rebecca," Sergeant Wilson said to Reverend Pease after the ceremony. "Yesterday she had them smiling for the first time in weeks, and today she quieted them down quicker than we ever could. She has a knack with babies, I'd have to say."

"Beth Clarke," replied Reverend Pease "was the mother of two young children until the smallpox epidemic."

"Oh, no—I'm sorry to hear this."

"Beth lost her husband and her five-year-old boys. She's been a lost soul ever since. After her husband's death, she became a recluse. I paid her a visit and asked her if she could help out here at the church, which she agreed to do. So now she cleans, sets up for services, does some cooking, and the like. But the sadness still lingers—will always be there, I suspect."

"Reverend, do you think she would be able to help us out with the girls while we're stationed here in Savannah? It would only be for a week or so. We can pay her, and she can stay at the campsite if she's willing to rough it."

"Let's ask her!" replied Reverend Pease, with a glimmer in his eye.

The church's wagon rolled into Company E's campsite later that day and was met by Private Diggs. Reverend Pease, holding the reins firmly in both hands, disarmed many a soldier's stare with his engaging smile. Seated next to him was Beth, wearing a straw bonnet and cradling a straw suitcase in her lap; her face mirroring the apprehension she felt deep within.

"Welcome to our camp!" said Private Diggs, as he took Beth's suitcase and helped her climb off the wagon.

"Thank ya'," whispered Beth.

The good reverend knew it would serve no purpose for him to stay around during the transition, so he waved at Beth and hollered out, "Good luck! I'll come visit you in just a few days."

Beth tentatively waved good-bye; off Reverend Pease rode, never looking back.

Beth was a bundle of nerves, and rightfully so. She initially resisted the idea, but Reverend Pease had talked her into it, just as he had coaxed Beth out of self-imposed isolation after her family's tragic demise. This would be Beth's first paying job as well as her first time living amongst white folk. She felt that she could trust Sergeant Wilson and Private Diggs, but she was unsure about all these other soldiers, some of whom were now staring and pointing toward her. The thought of sleeping in a tent at an army campsite, surrounded by guns and strange men, heightened her stress.

Beth's fears were put aside for the moment when two soldiers ran up to greet her with Mary and Becky bouncing atop their shoulders.

"Welcome, ma'm," said the private giving Becky a ride. "I think these here girls need some female influence. If they gotta' put up with us much longer, why, we'll turn em' into little boys!"

Beth smiled and held out her arms, which were quickly filled with smiling babies.

"We have the twins sleeping in a big ole' officer's tent and that's where you'll be staying too," said Private Diggs. "We gotta' cot in there and blankets for ya'. Breakfast is at six o'clock in the morning. I hope you don't mind bugle calls, cause we gotta' lot of that happenin' around here! Come, folla' me, I'll show ya' everything ya' need to know!"

Private Diggs took Mary from Beth's arms and began his guided tour of the campsite. Beth held onto Becky as she walked into a strange, new chapter of her life.

Chapter 7

Savannah, Tuesday

Captain Baker was furious. He paced back and forth in front of his tent as Sergeant Wilson and Private Diggs stood at attention, quietly listening to a litany of complaints disguised as rhetorical questions.

"Why didn't you tell me that this nonsense about the babies went all the way up to General Howard? Were you trying to hide something from me? Do you understand that my reputation is on the line here, dammit?"

Not knowing which question to answer first, Sergeant Wilson jumped in and tried his best.

"It wasn't our intention to hide anything from you, sir. We were given an ultimatum by the regimental surgeon. He told us either the twins are to be placed with a local family or we would have to drop them off at an orphanage. One way or another, we'll have this situation resolved by Friday. No disrespect intended, Captain Baker, we didn't think it would be necessary to trouble you with these trivial matters."

"When General Howard sends word that he needs to see me it's a damn sight more than a trivial matter!"

"We had no idea he would get involved!"

"Well he did—and now he's going to ask a lot of damn questions that I don't have good answers for."

"Yes sir, I understand now. Sorry, sir. This is all my fault. No harm was intended to anyone. If I knew the surgeon was taking this matter to General Howard I would have told you about it ahead of time."

"Sergeant Wilson, I need you to fetch those babies and take them to command headquarters, tomorrow morning, at 9:30 sharp. Wait out front, on the sidewalk, until I arrive. And don't say anything to anyone until I see you tomorrow morning. Is that understood?"

"Yes sir. But I believe that I'll need either Private Diggs or Beth to come with me, you know, to help out with handling the twins."

"Beth? Who the hell is Beth?"

"Beth is a local lady we just hired on to help care for the twins. We met her…"

Captain Baker held up his hand to silence Sergeant Wilson. His face reddened as he fought off the urge to scream into their faces; he barely managed to continue on in a subdued, but trembling, voice.

"Bring the twins, bring Private Diggs, and bring this Beth lady, too. I want to see all of you, tomorrow. Be waiting in front of command headquarters. Is that perfectly understood?"

"Yes sir."

"And keep your mouths shut about this matter—don't say anything to anyone about any of this."

"Yes sir," replied both Sergeant Wilson and Private Diggs.

An idle army, with fresh wages burning a hole in their pockets, turns to drinking, gambling, unmentionable vices, and thoughts of home and family. Many homesick soldiers requested a leave of absence so they could visit their parents, wives, and children. General Howard, who was busy planning his army's upcoming campaign, a northward thrust into the heart of the secessionist state of South Carolina, duly issued General Field Order No. 38:

> General Field Order No. 38
> Headquarters of the Department and
> Army of the Tennessee
> Savannah, Georgia, December 27, 1864
>
> The interests of the service demanding the presence of all efficient officers and men with their commands, in view of another short and decisive campaign, no leaves of absence or furloughs, except on surgeon's certificate of disability, or in extreme cases of family suffering and distress, will, for the present, be granted this command.
>
> By Order of Maj. Gen. O.O. Howard

Chapter 8

Savannah, Wednesday Morning

Major General Oliver Otis Howard, commander of the Army of the Tennessee, selected for his Savannah headquarters a well-appointed townhome in the tony City Park district of Savannah. To the victors belong the spoils.

Private Diggs, Beth, and the twins waited patiently on the sidewalk in front of the townhome. Above them, hanging on angled flag poles recently fastened to the facade of the building, were the stars and stripes and the flag of the Army of the Tennessee. Private Diggs held Rebecca, while Beth stood next to him, holding Mary.

Not as patient was Sergeant Wilson, who paced back and forth, mumbling under his breath, repeating over and over again the words he needed to say to Captain Baker.

The twins were busy chattering at each other in unintelligible baby talk. While in her care, Beth enjoyed talking to the twins. The topics of conversation hardly mattered: the weather, the clothes they were wearing, the toys they were playing with. Whatever came into Beth's mind, she shared with the girls. They soon started filling in voids in Beth's conversation with little conversations of their own.

Beth looked at a puzzled Private Diggs and remarked offhandedly, "I have no idea what they're chattering about, but I'm guessing they sure enough know."

"I sure enough hope they're telling each other to be on their best behavior in there," replied Private Diggs.

Captain Baker finally arrived. Sergeant Wilson intercepted the captain as he walked towards the group, and, with little hesitation, launched into his carefully rehearsed speech.

"Captain Baker, I wholeheartedly apologize for springing this on you at the last minute, but after careful consideration, my wife and I have decided that we would like to adopt the babies."

Captain Baker stared into Sergeant Wilson's eyes, trying to gauge his intentions.

"And I assume that you've communicated with your wife regarding this matter?" asked Captain Baker.

"I mailed her a letter, but haven't heard back yet."

"When did you post this letter?"

"Yesterday," Sergeant Wilson sheepishly confessed.

"This is an important commitment to be making without your wife's consent, is it not?"

"Yes sir, it is, but we only have a few more days to get this matter resolved, and it would break our hearts to drop these girls off at an orphanage considering all that they've been through."

Captain Baker was unexpectedly calm. He glanced over at the twins and became fixated on the bandage covering Mary's tiny finger.

"We'll see!" responded Captain Baker. Raising his voice so that all could hear, he added "Once we're inside, I'll do all the talking."

General Howard was a West Point graduate, a seasoned soldier, a vocal abolitionist, and a devout Christian. He fought for the Union army from the very onset of the war, at the First Battle of Bull Run; he lost his right arm during the Battle of Fair Oaks; he commanded a division at the bloody Battle of Antietam that suffered over two thousand casualties; he became field commander during the first day of the Battle of Gettysburg after General Reynolds fell victim to a rebel sharpshooter; and he was hand-picked by General Sherman to command the southern wing of the Union army during his history-making Savannah Campaign.

The general also had a soft spot in his heart for little children.

On cue from an orderly, Captain Baker entered General Howard's tiny office.

"Come in—all of you—I want everyone in here," summoned the general, from behind his oversized and cluttered desk.

Captain Baker looked back into the hallway and whispered "Beth, hand the baby to Sergeant Wilson and you can wait out here."

"No—everyone come into my office. I want to see all of you," the general insisted.

General Howard's cramped office suddenly became very crowded.

"So these are the babies I've heard all about? Let me hold one of 'em."

The general spun his desk chair around and held out his left arm; Beth, who was closest, handed Mary over to him. She gently placed Mary on the left side of the general's lap, so that he could cradle the baby with his only arm.

"And what are their names?" asked a smiling General Howard. Captain Baker looked towards Sergeant Wilson for the answer.

"You're holding Mary, sir, and Private Diggs has Rebecca," responded Sergeant Wilson.

"And Mary is the one wounded in battle, I see?" General Howard asked while holding up and inspecting Mary's bandaged little finger.

"Yes, sir—the tip of her finger was taken away," replied Sergeant Wilson. Captain Baker gave Sergeant Wilson a cold stare; with that comment he was, in the captain's opinion, ignoring orders not to speak.

"Well then, little lady," the general said to Mary in a soft voice, "it appears we share something in common, don't we—my missing arm and your missing fingertip! I guess this makes you a war veteran!"

Mary looked up into the general's bushy black beard and cooed.

A smiling general asked Captain Baker, "So how was it that these two babies came to be traveling through battlefields with your company?"

"Well, sir, if I may explain," responded Captain Baker, somewhat nervously. "We found them in a life-threatening situation. They were trapped inside a railroad coaling station we had just put the torch to, and they were rescued by these here two soldiers, Sergeant Wilson and Private Diggs. We canvassed the area but no families had heard of these babies and no one was willing to take them in. So we brought them here, to Savannah, and now we'll either place them with a local family or in an orphanage. Our deadline is this Friday. One way or the other, sir, this matter will be resolved by Friday."

"And exactly how did little Mary come to lose her fingertip?" queried the general, as he held Mary's tiny hand up into the air for all to see.

"It was about two weeks ago. We were back in Low Country, in the middle of swamp land. There was an early morning attack by rebel cavalry, just as we were breaking down the campsite. We were in the wrong place at the wrong time, general—the rebs were retreating, and we were in their way. An unfortunate event, all around, I'd have to say."

"All casualties are unfortunate events. But casualties such as this should never happen, and will never happen again—not under my command. Babies do not belong in the care of armies during wartime. If the press should get hold of this story we'll be the laughingstock of the Northern newspapers and vilified in Richmond's newspapers. We cannot allow that to happen!"

"Yes sir."

"Sir, may I speak?" requested Sergeant Wilson.

"Speak your mind, Sergeant," responded the general.

Captain Baker silently fumed.

"We would much prefer to place these babies with a good family rather than drop them off at an orphanage. Time's a-wastin' and we just don't know where to start with finding them a proper home here in Savannah. If I could just have a two-week furlough, I can take the babies up to my home in Indiana, and my wife would care for 'em there, sir."

"It appears that you've grown quite fond of these babies, haven't you?" asked the general.

"Yes sir, all three of us have." The sergeant paused, then added, "That is, Private Diggs and I have, I meant to say. They've been with us for about a month now, and we treat 'em like our own daughters."

The general smiled and nodded his head; but his hands were tied, bound by his own General Field Order No. 38.

"You're dismissed, ladies and men."

Chapter 9

Savannah, Wednesday Afternoon

There were seven of them in on the plan, and it was a risky one at that. A sergeant, a corporal, and five privates banded together for a common cause: get the babies safely out of Savannah.

Early afternoon found them all at Savannah's Female Orphan Asylum.

"Who's in charge of this facility?" demanded Sergeant Wilson. The receptionist was startled by the sudden appearance of a half dozen Union soldiers, who entered the lobby and formed a semicircle around her, all standing at attention. It was intended to be a menacing sight, and it was.

"I'll fetch Nurse Anderson," she replied in a shaky voice; she then quickly disappeared through a door leading into the children's wards.

Moments later, an elderly nurse entered the lobby and stood defiantly in front of them.

"What is the meaning of this?" she demanded.

"We intend no harm, Nurse Anderson," replied Sergeant Wilson, "but we need your help. Can you issue adoption papers for two orphan girls we found back in Georgia? We figured this'd be the best place to get 'em."

"You want me to forge adoption papers?"

"I guess so, ma'm."

"And if I decide to cooperate, what is it you plan on doing with these children?"

"We need to transport two innocent one-year-old girls as far away as possible from this godforsaken war. I'll be taking them to a good home, up in Indiana—my home."

"And where are these children right now?"

"They're waiting outside—would you like to meet them?"

"Bring them in, I don't have all day, you know."

"Yes ma'm."

One of the men broke ranks, opened the front door, waved, and in walked Private Diggs with Rebecca and Mary cradled in his arms. The girls had been bathed and dressed in their best clothes. Beth had tied red ribbons into their hair.

Nurse Anderson was taken aback by the babies' affluent appearance.

"And who is to be the adoption mother and father?" she asked.

"My wife and I," said Sergeant Wilson.

"Where is your wife?"

"Back home, in Indiana."

"We'll need her signature too, you realize, for it to be a legal adoption."

"Well then, we'll just have to make this an illegal one."

Nurse Anderson stared at Sergeant Wilson for a moment, slowly sat down in the receptionist's desk chair, and drew a deep breath.

"These girls look better cared for than most of the children in Savannah, orphaned or otherwise. I believe you men are sincere in your intentions, but you are asking me to break a law, the law being what it is these days. So, may I ask, what will this orphanage receive in return for adoption papers?"

Sergeant Wilson looked perplexed.

"I'm not understanding you, ma'm. What is it you need us to do?"

"A simple request, Sergeant—a barter deal, would best describe it. You see, this orphanage was built to house seventy-five female children and we presently have over twice that number in our care. We're low on food, clothing, soap, bedding, medical supplies—just about every resource needed to care for the children. Now your conquering Union army possesses all these valuable resources. All we need is for you to share them with us."

"Well ma'm, I can't speak for the entire Union army, but we'll do our damnedest to help you out. Rations have been good here in Savannah—we can share food with you. And we've recently been paid—we can take up a collection, too."

"Talk is cheap! Show me what you can do for the orphanage and maybe you'll earn your adoption papers."

The soldiers stared at each other; a few began looking aimlessly around, shifting their weight uneasily from one foot to the other. This wasn't part of the plan.

Sergeant Wilson led the way and a few of the others quickly took the cue. Eventually, all were digging deep into their uniform pockets.

Chapter 10

Savannah, Thursday Evening

All the plan's details had been carefully worked out.

Beth would be needed to help care for the twins during their long journey northward. She was up to the task, but it wasn't safe for a person of color to travel through areas of conflict. The gang of seven proposed various schemes, and after some debate they reached a consensus. Beth had freedom papers, which she would carry with her; nevertheless, Sergeant Wilson would insinuate, but not say definitively, that Beth was his property. This would allow them the flexibility, depending on the situation at hand, for Beth to play the role of a free person or a slave. This was the best course of action they could think of.

Sergeant Wilson was also at risk, as he would be AWOL for two weeks or longer, in direct conflict with General Field Order No. 38. Union soldiers have been executed for such offenses. The sergeant was leaning heavily on leniency owing to extenuating circumstances, and also in consideration of their somewhat favorable visit with General Howard. It was a high stakes gamble, but Sergeant Wilson was willing to take it.

That evening they all sat around a campfire, quietly reviewing the final stages of their plan. Civilian clothes and suitcases had been purchased for Sergeant Wilson with what little money they had left after donating over fifty U.S. green-backs to the orphanage. Sergeant Wilson would be traveling with only sixty dollars in his pocket, which represented three months of his sergeant's pay. There was talk of taking up a company-wide collection to help spread out the expenditures, but it was decided that, in order to maintain secrecy, all details of the plan had to stay within the group of seven.

The plan was for Sergeant Wilson to dress up in his newly purchased suit and slip out of camp early Friday morning, before dawn, with Beth and the girls. Thunderbolt Landing was due east of Savannah, too far to walk, and pilfering an army wagon was out of the question; and so it was arranged that they would walk to the nearest road where Reverend Pease would meet them with the church's wagon and drive them there. Reverend Pease would wait while steamship tickets were being purchased. If for any reason a ticket north to either Baltimore or Washington could not be purchased, then the entire mission would have to be cancelled.

Sergeant Wilson would play the role of a successful businessman escorting his children to his parent's home in Indiana in order to spare them the hardships of the Union army's occupation of Savannah. He would pose as a trans-planted Northerner because his Southern accent, as he was told over and over again by his co-conspirators, was poor and unbelievable. If the situation hadn't been so dire there would have been great teasing and mirth over the sergeant's futile attempts to imitate a Southern drawl.

Nobody knew for sure when General Howard's army would be marching out of Savannah, and this complicated matters terribly. Word had already spread among the enlisted soldiers that soon after the New Year, General Howard's wing would spearhead the Union army's thrust into central South Carolina. Soldiers stationed on the east side of Savannah near Warsaw Sound reported that steamships were arriving and preparing to transport troops northward to places unknown. If the army should be on the move during the upcoming weeks, and the newspapers failed to report on their exact movements, then Sergeant Wilson's AWOL duration would be extended and his life would surely be in greater peril.

Sergeant Wilson thought about all this, and the gravity of the situation began to wear on him. He excused himself from the campfire meeting and visited with Beth and the twins before retiring. While holding his sleeping daughters, he asked Beth if she was fully aware of the dangers they might encounter during the journey to Indiana. Beth paused for a moment, deep in thought, and then replied, "There are many, many things in this world that I'm afraid of. This ain't one of them."

"Thank you" was all Sergeant Wilson could manage to say.

That evening, Sergeant Wilson lay awake, tossing and turning on his army cot. Brief but vivid dreams ranged from his wife tenderly cradling their daughters to the horror of facing a firing squad. At 2:00 a.m., he accepted the fact that he was not going to be able to sleep that night. He lay on his cot, face up, staring into the darkness.

And then he heard a loud, firm voice from just outside his tent. "Sergeant Ezekiel Wilson, we need to speak with you at once!"

Sergeant Wilson quickly put his trousers on, one suspender up and the other dangling, and opened his tent's front flap. A young, baby-faced lieutenant and two privates armed with Springfield rifles stood outside.

"Get the rest of your clothes on and come with us!" the lieutenant ordered.

"Am I under arrest?" Sergeant Wilson asked in a shaky voice.

"I'm not at liberty to say—just do as you're told. And be quick about it."

The ride into downtown Savannah seemingly took forever. The wagon came to a halt directly in front of the flag of the Army of the Tennessee. A lump formed deep within Sergeant Wilson's throat.

Sergeant Wilson was escorted into headquarters and ordered to sit on a bench in the outer hallway. The privates were dismissed, and the lieutenant sat down on another bench at the opposite end of the hallway. Only a few rooms were illuminated and the building was quiet, in stark contrast to Sergeant Wilson's first visit. They sat waiting for fifteen minutes, at which point Sergeant Wilson could no longer contain himself.

"Could you please tell me why I've been brought here? Am I in any kind of trouble?"

"I'm not privy to these matters, so I can't answer your questions, Sergeant. But it can't be a good thing, now, can it?"

"I suppose not," was Sergeant Wilson's mumbled response.

Just then a door opened and a colonel appeared; he motioned for Sergeant Wilson to enter into his office. As Sergeant Wilson tried to stand up, a leg buckled; he caught himself by placing a hand against the wall.

Once inside the room, which appeared to have once been a well-appointed study but now served as office space for General Howard's staff, the colonel motioned for Sergeant Wilson to be seated on a straight-backed chair in the corner of the room. He gently closed the door, and then stood at the center of the room. He hovered there for a few seconds, staring at Sergeant Wilson, before speaking.

"What are we supposed to do with deserters like you?" asked the colonel.

"I'm not a deserter, sir."

"But you intend to be! We have sworn testimony from two men of your company that you were ready to leave camp in the morning and head back to your home in Indiana. That's desertion, Sergeant! Is my account not factual?" Sergeant Wilson paused for a moment, weighing the consequences of an honest answer versus a misleading one. He decided honesty would work best under these dire circumstances.

"Yes, sir. That is what I was planning to do, but you see it was just to be for two or three weeks, in order to get some important personal business taken care of. If I'd have…"

"Quiet!" demanded the colonel, but in a hushed tone of voice.

"Yes, sir!"

"If it were up to me you'd be facing stern disciplinary action. But you're a very lucky fellow—General Howard has taken a personal interest in this case."

The colonel grabbed a signed document off a desktop and handed it to Sergeant Wilson. His hands trembling, Sergeant Wilson held the paper chest-high and began to read.

Headquarters of the Department and
Army of the Tennessee
Savannah, Georgia, December 29, 1864

Sergeant Ezekiel Wilson, 83rd Regiment, Company E, shall be granted a two-week furlough for purpose of escorting a convalescing honorary Union soldier to her home in Indiana.

By Order of Maj. Gen. O. O. Howard

Chapter 11

Central Indiana, Christmas Eve, 1888

Uncle Zeke was now two hours into his story. For the most part, he sat stoically and spoke in a matter-of-fact manner. But this quickly changed when the emotions he felt that early morning, twenty-four years ago, after reading General Howard's order, were rekindled. Tears welled up in his eyes. Uncle Zeke found a clean edge on his dinner napkin and gently dabbed it in the corners of his eyes.

"General Howard," Uncle Zeke said, after regaining composure, "has the heart of a lion and the soul of a just and righteous man."

He paused to fold his napkin and place it on the table.

"Back there in Savannah, he didn't have to do anything for me—for us—but he made an effort to ensure our safety and well-being. After the war, when General Howard was heading up the Freedmen's Bureau, I sent him a letter thanking him for his kindness that day. The general took the time to write a letter in response."

Uncle Zeke picked up his kepi hat and took out a folded piece of paper from inside the hat's crown. He handed it to Mary.

"Please Mary, you read it—I don't have my reading glasses handy."

Mary unfolded the paper while staring at Uncle Zeke. It was a brief, handwritten note, on plain stationary that was once white, but now yellowed with age.

Washington, D.C.
Mar 29th, 1866

Sergeant Ezekiel Wilson:

It brings me much joy to hear that you survived the war and are sharing your home and Christian faith with the two young ladies you introduced to me at Savannah H.Q. May God bless and protect you and your family.

Very truly yours,
Maj. Gen. O. O. Howard
Maj. Gen. U.S. Army

Chapter 12

Central Indiana, January 7, 1865

It had been a smooth journey northward for Sergeant Wilson, Beth and the twins.

In addition to furlough papers duly drawn up by Captain Baker, Sergeant Wilson also carried with him General Howard's handwritten order. These documents ensured first-class treatment by all who came in contact with them.

Wartime railroad service was erratic, but limited train schedules did not significantly impede their progress. At Thunderbolt Landing, they boarded an empty supply ship that brought them to Washington, DC. This was the riskiest leg of their journey, but the steamship ride was without incident. In Washington, DC they switched to a passenger train taking them to Chicago, and at Chicago Union Station, they transferred to a train bound for Indianapolis. At Indianapolis Union Depot, they boarded a rickety, old Peru & Indianapolis Railroad passenger train that brought them to their final destination. It was while riding this train that they heard the news.

Sergeant Wilson began to notice that their train was nearly empty while stations on the opposite track, for trains heading to Indianapolis, were overflowing with people, mostly whole families, patiently waiting for the next train to arrive. He was puzzled by this. An elderly gentleman with smartly coiffured white hair boarded the train at one such station and sat toward the rear of their car. After observing him for a while, Sergeant Wilson decided to walk back and strike up a conversation.

"Good day, sir. May I introduce myself? I'm Ezekiel Wilson."

"Good afternoon, Ezekiel, I'm Dr. Cornelius Adams. I'm pleased to make your acquaintance. Heading home on leave, I assume?"

"I'm on a two-week furlough, sir—bringing my adopted daughters back home."

"Very nice! I've been sitting here watching them play with their nanny. I must say they are well-spirited and well-behaved."

"Thank you, sir."

"So where's your home?"

"It's the next stop. I can't wait to see my wife again. It's been over a year since I've been home."

"Have you heard from your wife lately?"

"Why, no, I've not received a letter from her in a bit over a month now, which is a bit unusual."

"Well I don't want to overly concern you, Ezekiel, but this region is in the middle of a smallpox outbreak. I'm just now heading to your town, to lend some assistance."

Sergeant Wilson was stunned. His mind began to race with thoughts of Gertrude and family. He also wondered how he was going to break this news to Beth.

"Doctor, do you have someone meeting you at the train station?" Ezekiel asked.

"Yes, I do."

"May I ask a tall favor of you? If there's enough room for all of us, and if it's not too far out of your way, would you please take us over to my home, just in case my wife should need some medical attention?"

"It sounds like the wise thing to do. We can make that happen, Sergeant."

No one responded to Ezekiel's knock at the front door. While Beth held the twins tighter than ever, and Dr. Adams and his driver waited patiently in the wagon, Ezekiel circled his home and peeked into each window as he passed by. It was through their bedroom window's parted curtains that he finally spotted Gertrude, in bed, fast asleep. His sister-in-law Beatrice was with her; she was sitting in a rocking chair and had dozed off while reading a book. Ezekiel gently tapped on the window pane. Beatrice looked up with a puzzled expression; and then her face lit up with excitement when she recognized her brother-in-law.

"Thank you, Lord" she shouted as she ran to open the front door.

Beatrice and Beth fussed over the twins while Ezekiel sat in his favorite easy chair by the fireplace for the first time in over a year. He would have enjoyed the experience more if his mind wasn't spinning with thoughts of Gertrude's condition and his daughters' future.

Dr. Adams emerged from the bedroom and announced the findings of his examination.

"Well I have some good news. She doesn't have smallpox."

Both Ezekiel and Beatrice let out a collective sigh of relief. Beth let out a faint "Hallelujah."

Then Dr. Adams turned towards Beatrice.

"You're her sister, do I have that right?"

"Yes, doctor, I'm her sister—my name is Beatrice."

"I'm pleased to make your acquaintance. Beatrice, were you and your sister raised here in town or out in the countryside?"

"We lived on a farm about twenty miles due west of here. Our parents own a small farm."

"That's fine. And did this farm have dairy cows when you and Gertrude were children?"

"We had two milking cows."

"Very good. And can you ever remember coming down with a sickness they call cowpox?"

"Yes, I had cowpox when I was twelve years old."

"And your sister—did she ever have cowpox?"

"I cannot recall. She's nine years younger than me, and I left home when I was sixteen years old, when I married, and so we were out of touch for quite a while."

"Thank you, you've been a great help. Well, my examination is complete. I'm not exactly sure what your sister is suffering from, but, based on her symptoms—fatigue, anxiety, and severe headaches—I suspect she has developed a condition called neurasthenia. This is a fancy word that simply means she's overstressed her central nervous system. We're seeing more and more of this condition since the war began. Bed rest, a healthy diet, and solitude would be the best medicine for your sister. And keep her here at home, away from strangers, at least until this smallpox epidemic quiets down."

"Yes, doctor, we can certainly do that," responded a smiling Beatrice.

"Smallpox is an unpredictable disease—some of us are immune while others are highly vulnerable. Beatrice, I believe that you are not at risk. Nevertheless, be very careful over the next few months."

"Yes doctor, I'll do that."

"And that advice goes for all of you. Now, I must take leave—I have patients waiting at the infirmary."

With that, elderly Dr. Adams, the compassionate country doctor, said his good-byes and left.

Plans were hastily revised.

Beth would not travel back to Savannah with Ezekiel; she agreed it would be best to delay her trip home until Gertrude was back on her feet. Beth and the twins would stay at the Wilson's home, and Beth would assist Beatrice with Gertrude's convalescence. Beth and Beatrice would share responsibility for the twins' care.

Once Beth settled in and gained the confidence of Gertrude, Beatrice would be able to spend more time at home with her husband, Isaac, who missed her dearly. But until then, the walls of the Wilson home would be their shelter from the storm that was a deadly smallpox epidemic.

Ezekiel, who had allowed Dr. Adams to examine Gertrude before making his visit home known to her, gently opened the bedroom door and peeked in. Gertrude was still in bed, but sitting up. She was staring blankly out of the bedroom window.

"Gertie," he said softly.

Gertrude became startled. When she turned to see who had called her name, she still wore a blank expression. Then her face softened.

"Zeke, you're back from the war! Come over here and give me a big hug!"

Ezekiel ran to her side, hugged her tight, and sat down next to her.

"Are you home for good?"

"No Gertie, I'll be here for a very short time. I have a two-week furlough, and if I don't hop back on a train soon, I'll be late getting back to camp. But I had to come home to see you and tell you the news."

"What news, Zeke? Have you been injured?"

"No Gertie, I'm fine. It's just that…"

"I fear so much that you will be harmed, Zeke! The newspapers print these awful lists of soldiers' names. I read through them almost every day."

"Yes, I know, Gertie. But look at me, I'm fine!"

She stared into Ezekiel's eyes, but there was no connection; her eyes appeared listless and dull. Perhaps she was fighting inward demons and they were getting the best of her, Ezekiel thought. Doctor Adams's prescription, "…bed rest, a healthy diet and solitude …," kept resonating over and over again in his mind.

"What is the news you came to tell me?" asked Gertrude.

"It's just that… it's that…we're winning the war and soon I'll be home for good. Real soon, I'd expect!"

An hour later, Ezekiel emerged from the bedroom and all eyes were cast upon him.

"What did she say?" asked Beatrice in a soft tone of voice.

"Say about what?"

"What did she say about the babies, Zeke?" she asked, this time a bit louder.

"She doesn't know yet," he solemnly replied.

After a brief stay, Ezekiel packed his bag and walked to the train station. Inside the Wilson home, Beatrice and Beth heard the train's whistle blow as it pulled out of town; they paused for just a moment to glance at each other before resuming the chores at hand.

A home once quiet save for the creaking of floorboards and the hushed tones of adult conversation was now a bee-hive of activity. At first Beatrice attended to her bedridden sister while Beth looked after the twins, but as weeks passed, they began sharing these responsibilities. Beatrice ran all the household errands, splitting her time away between markets and visiting with Isaac.

The twins began to walk, and it seemed as though they were learning to speak new words each day. They were sisters and best friends and would play together for hours on end. The loudest noise they made was gleeful laughter; a welcome sound in the troubled Wilson home.

Beth began to feel the effects of cabin fever, and so she asked Beatrice if she could go to market every now and then, just to break up the day. But her first and only visit to a local produce market proved unnerving; she was stared at and could sense that townspeople were talking about her behind her back. It is peculiar, Beth thought, that she had traveled all the way up North, to the land of abolitionists and freedom fighters, only to be gazed upon as an object of curiosity. After that bad experience, Beth suggested that Beatrice run all of the household errands.

Just as Gertrude began to recover from her bout of neuras-thenia, Isaac's health began to fail. Beatrice was beside herself with worry, and she could not sleep on most nights. Gertrude swapped roles with Beatrice and became her caregiver.

Beth visited with Isaac on those days when Beatrice could not muster up the energy to get out of bed. Eventually Isaac was transported to the town's makeshift infirmary and placed under the care of Dr. Adams.

Chapter 13

Central Indiana, Christmas Eve, 1888

"I made my way back to the train station, leaving behind a mess of a situation here at home. I know now that it was a crazy plan I hatched, but the war, the desperate situation we were in, well, I guess it just got the best of me and I wasn't thinking straight."

Mary interrupted, "No, Uncle Zeke, it wasn't a crazy plan at all! It was a wonderful plan, a beautiful plan!"

"Yes it was!" added Becky. "First you saved our lives, then you took us under your wing and protected us, and then you gave us a home and a loving mother. Don't you ever say it was a crazy plan!"

"Thank you" was all Uncle Zeke could manage to say, in a subdued voice.

The mantle clock struck midnight. All waited for the twelfth and final chime to sound before wishing each other a Merry Christmas. What followed then was awkward silence.

Mary spoke first. "Uncle Zeke, we need you to finish the story."

Uncle Zeke cleared his throat and said "I would imagine, at this point, that you can fill in the rest of it all by yourselves."

"Please go on, Uncle Zeke. Don't stop now!" pleaded Becky.

"Well, I arrived back at camp two days late but nobody seemed to care much about that. They had promoted Private Diggs to corporal while I was gone, so I guess we didn't make Captain Baker all that upset with our shenanigans. But the entire company was in a depressed state of mind. We had been doing something so special for so long, but then, after you girls went up north, we were just another bunch of soldiers fightin' in General Sherman's army. It was as though we had lost our purpose, our identity."

"A few days later, we broke camp and moved out of Savannah—the South Carolina Campaign had finally begun and we were right in the thick of it. General Howard's entire wing was taken by transport steamships to Beaufort, in South Carolina, and from there we began our march inland, towards the city of Columbia. The fightin' was fierce."

"Then, after a month or so went by, I received a letter from Aunt Gertrude with the bad news about your father."

Uncle Zeke gave a quick, uneasy glance toward Aunt Gertrude.

"Then about three weeks later, I received another letter with the bad news about Beth."

There was a collective gasp from Mary, Becky and Robert.

"She died? Of smallpox?" Mary asked.

"Yes, she did," responded Aunt Gertrude. "Beth volunteered to help Beatrice care for your father. She must have believed herself not at risk after surviving the epidemic in Savannah. But, I guess…"

Aunt Gertrude paused and shook her head slowly; her eyes began to tear up, and a tiny tear trickled down her cheek.

Uncle Zeke jumped in and said, "She was a brave woman to have gone through what she went through with her own family, and then turn around and do all that she did for our family."

"Amen," whispered Aunt Gertrude.

"And this was when mother decided to adopt us?" asked Mary.

"Yep, it was just like Aunt Gertrude said earlier," Uncle Zeke responded. "You little angels filled up a big hole in Beatrice's heart. You gave her reason to carry on in life."

Aunt Gertrude quickly interjected, "I would have taken you girls in myself, but Beatrice needed you so much more. And, to tell the honest truth, I wasn't in a state of mind back then to care for little babies. For years after the war, I struggled mightily with that neurasthenia."

After saying this, Aunt Gertrude's head tilted downward and her shoulders slumped. It was as if a heavy weight had just been lifted off of her.

Mary stood up, quickly walked behind Aunt Gertrude and placed her hands on her aunt's shoulders. "I understand. You did what was best for all of us—you did everything as best you possibly could," she said.

"So much could have turned out differently. I just wish that…" Aunt Gertrude's voice trailed off, and a second tear slowly worked its way down her other cheek. She never finished the sentence; it was a thought she never could nor would be able to verbalize.

Mary stood behind Aunt Gertrude, gently rubbing on her shoulders. Aunt Gertrude looked back at her and softly smiled through tear-filled eyes.

Becky asked, "There's one last mystery. What about that second adoption, the one in Jeffersonville? How did father's name come to be on those adoption papers?"

Uncle Zeke let out a sly smile. "We were afraid that they wouldn't allow a widower to adopt little babies—so I pretended I was your father."

"Goodness gracious! You mean to say we were adopted twice, and both times it was illegal?"

"Like your aunt already said," replied Uncle Zeke, "they're just documents—nothing but a bunch of legal gibberish."

Mary and Becky both let out a chuckle.

"So is there anything else you can possibly tell us tonight, Uncle Zeke?" asked Mary.

"Not now," responded Uncle Zeke, "but I'd like you all to meet me at Sycamore Hill Cemetery tomorrow morning before church. I've got some unfinished business to attend to."

Chapter 14

Central Indiana, Christmas Morning, 1888

Christmas morning presented Indianans with the gift of sunlight and milder weather. A thin blanket of snow covered the area's patch quilt of farm fields; an early morning sun sat low on the horizon, casting a bright orange glow onto nature's canvas of pure, white snow.

Uncle Zeke and Aunt Gertrude separately exited their carriage, merged into one, and walked through the wrought iron front gate of Sycamore Hill Cemetery. Mary, Becky and Robert, standing alongside Beatrice and Isaac's graves, watched as the couple slowly made their way up the hill. Uncle Zeke was carrying his old kepi hat, and his other arm was wrapped about Aunt Gertrude's waist. They appeared calm and content; almost happy, in spite of the solemn occasion.

"They look at peace," said Becky.

"Yes, I believe they are," replied Mary.

After Christmas wishes were exchanged, Uncle Zeke said, "On the ride out this morning, Aunt Gertrude and I were talking about how God must have created a special place in heaven for mothers like Beatrice."

All nodded and smiled in response.

While they looked on, Uncle Zeke removed a small piece of paper from his overcoat's inner pocket. It was General Howard's handwritten letter.

"The good general sent this letter to me, but he didn't write this letter for me. This is your mother's letter."

The folded, yellowed paper was placed on Beatrice's grave. Uncle Zeke carefully covered it with some loose dirt and then placed a small rock on top of it.

Uncle Zeke dusted the soil off his hands and said, "Please follow me. We'll have to walk a bit, though."

With puzzled looks, everyone fell in line behind Uncle Zeke. At first, it seemed he knew where he was heading, but then he started to meander back and forth in many directions, as if lost. After walking through an old section of the cemetery for a few minutes, he stopped, bent down, and dusted the snow off the ground with his bare hand; but there was an expression of disappointment. He glanced to his immediate right and swiped again at a thin layer of white snow.

"Here we go!" said Uncle Zeke as he stood up and smiled. "Come see this."

Aunt Gertrude stood fast while Mary, Becky and Robert eased in closer.

> Beth Clarke
> b. Unknown
> d. 27 Feb 1865

"She had to be buried here in the colored section of the cemetery, but I know she wasn't turned away from that special place in heaven. And now she has Beatrice to keep her company."

Mary and Becky stared down at the grave marker, struggling to contain their emotions.

Uncle Zeke placed his old kepi hat atop Beth's grave marker and turned toward them.

"Last night, after you all left, I took my uniform off and tossed it into the fireplace. It made a spectacular fire."

Mary and Becky looked at Uncle Zeke, but not a word was said. Uncle Zeke bent down and adjusted the hat's position, ever so carefully, so that Beth's entire name could be read. He arose, dusting the snow off his hands.

"I'm done fighting the war now. Gertie, let's go home."

Afterword

Some of the most compelling Civil War stories may be found in firsthand personal accounts written after the war ended. The fictional story you just read is based upon events described in the following narrative:

> Military Order of the Loyal Legion of the United States, Commandery of the District of Columbia
>
> War Papers No. 28 – Recollections of a Bummer
>
> Prepared by Companion Major Charles E. Belknap, Late U.S.V. and Read at the Stated Meeting of January 5, 1898

Major Belknap tells of finding "two wee bits of girls," covered in grim and nearly dead from starvation and neglect, in a poverty-stricken area a few days march out of Atlanta. They were "shy as young partridges," but food won them over. A dozen local cabins were visited but "none could care for these motherless girls." The babies were washed, fed, and clothed, after which one of the soldiers described them as "just too sweet for anything."

The girls were "toted on the backs of soldiers" all the way to Savannah, where officials in that city were notified of the situation but said that they had no sympathy for "the little white trash." A wounded Union lieutenant was granted a furlough; he took them home with him, where they "reside today in happy homes, beautiful in their motherhood."